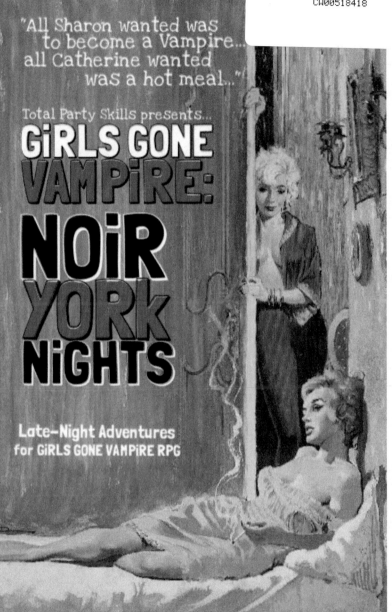

"All Sharon wanted was to become a Vampire... all Catherine wanted was a hot meal..."

Total Party Skills presents...

# GiRLS GONE VAMPiRE: NOiR YORK NiGHTS

Late-Night Adventures
for GiRLS GONE VAMPiRE RPG

# GiRLS GONE VAMPIRE: NOiR YORk NiGHTS

By Total Party Skills

Late Night Adventures for Girls Gone Vampire
Written by R. Joshua Holland
Cover and Interior Images via Public Domain
Copyright 2023

# THESE CURIOUS PLEASURES

by
**SLOANE
BRITAIN**

# tABLE Of CONtENtS

GOLD
MEDAL
BOOK

35¢

# ANN BANNON

Author of I AM A WOMAN

# WOMEN
# IN THE
# SHADOWS

Their dark and
troubled loves could
flourish only in secret

# Introduction

Adventures in GiRLS GONE VAMPiRE can take many familiar forms, drawing inspiration from classic horror stories, film noir murder-mysteries, crime thrillers, and occult fantasies. However, central to what makes GiRLS GONE VAMPiRE unique is its themes of forbidden lifestyles and slow-burn romance. Traditional style adventures where Characters are told about a thing, and go to find that thing and fight some cannon-fodder baddies along the way, and such quests can certainly be conceived for this Setting, but the intended style of play is for Characters to develop personal interests and relationships with the NPCs they encounter, and tease out the mysteries of Noir York City as they go.

The Adventures presented in this Sourcebook are designed for Low-Level Characters of different Vampire Cults, to introduce them to the world of GiRLS GONE VAMPiRE, and some of the notable figures they can encounter within it:

"COUNTERFEIT COMPANION"
A "talent scout" in the Inner Circle of Aoede has unorthodox methods and ulterior motives...

"INSATIABLE"
A newly created Vampire has escaped to hunt the city streets leaving a trail of bodies in her wake...

"GUTTER STAR"
Polyhymnia has her sights on taking an up-and-coming actress under wing...

"THE INCREDIBLE TRUTH"
A pair of Were-Cats threatens to betray their Society by bringing a Druidess into their secret rituals...

"UNNATURAL"
A Were-Cat has entered the Inner Circle of Clio to gain access to her collection of priceless artifacts...

"SPRING FIRE"
A sacrifice must be secured for the Vernal Equinox, but their father has a certain set of skills...

Each adventure synopsis includes relevant NPCs, Locations, and Encounters, as well as tips for using the adventure for Initiate or Vampire Player Characters. Many of these NPCs and Locations can be reused in any ongoing Campaign set in Noir York City.

These six adventures also serve to establish several important NPCs among Noir York's vampire community, as well as locations that can be used for other adventuring and encounter purposes.

Noir York Nights requires the "Girls Gone Vampire" Campaign Setting and the "Total Party System Rules Handbook" to make full use of.

PYRAMID BOOKS R-863 50¢

THE UNSPOKEN SECRET
OF A TWILIGHT LOVE

# STRANGE FRIENDS

AGNETE HOLK

## BOEOTIAN PENTHOUSE CLUB:

# "Counterfeit Companion"

Amanda Bryce has risen swiftly through the ranks of the Inner Circle of the Psychic Vampire, Aoede, and is known throughout the Penthouse Club as one of the best "talent scouts" for finding fresh young artists, full of potential and blood. She has not only procured several of her mistress' last few victims, but the demand for her services from other Psychic Vampires has made her a valuable asset for Aoede, to gain leverage or favor with her vampire sisters.

Her "talent" for talent-scouting is simple: she is a minor Druidess in the Cult of the Horned Goddess, and uses her dual status to find young wannabe artists, poets, and musicians among the cultists. She has ruthlessly sacrificed people who trusted in her, all in the hope that she could impress Aoede enough that she would grant Amanda the "gift" of vampiric immortality, unaware that to do so would destroy her mind and soul.

She could face dire consequences if she is discovered on either side. The Penthouse Club is cautious about the pagan followers of the legendary Vampire Tree that the Druidesses worship, while the Druidesses would react harshly not only to the betrayal of one of their number, but to the potential exposure of their inner secrets to the Boeotians.

The trouble begins when the latest artist Amanda procured for Aoede dies from a heroin overdose before Aoede could finish feeding upon him. Richard Barrister, a radio tycoon who bought his way onto Aoede's Inner Circle, will look for someone to keep tabs on Amanda, and make sure she finds a proper replacement so that her mistress can feed again as soon as possible.

Amanda will have to find someone who is already close to having an artistic breakthrough, and get them to go to Aoede's penthouse apartment so they can be inspired to finish their work quickly, and then be fed upon and discarded.

Amanda has someone in mind, but the girl in question is favored by some of the higher ranking Druidesses in her Cult. And with "someone" (the

Player Characters) trailing her, her double-life can all too easily be exposed.

Amanda's target is a folk singer and guitarist, who has been working on a composition for the Summer Solstice celebration, named Kelly Kyle. If she suddenly disappears, her Druidess girlfriend, Gretchen, will send an Initiate skilled with clairvoyance, along with a pair of beatnik followers, to track Kelly Kyle down.

Aoede is many centuries old, and will begin to lose her mind within a matter of months, instead of years as it is with younger Psychic Vampires who fail to drain their victim's sanity. She has had enough blood that her body will remain intact for quite some time, but the unexpected demise of her victim has made her retreat to her rooms to prevent her subordinates from seeing her rage.

Richard Barrister knows his position in the Penthouse Club is tenuous, and that it will likely disappear if something happened to Aoede that removed her from the cult. Hence his interest in having "someone" make sure that Amanda finds someone quick who suits Aoede's needs.

# Locations:

AOEDE'S PENTHOUSE:
The Vampire Aoede keeps her lair, and her private court, in a sprawling penthouse condominium that takes up the entire top floor of Rosenvale Tower, which overlooks Center Park from its northern end. Many of Aoede's personal entourage and Inner Circle will come and go from her Penthouse as they please, and she occassionally hosts private parties to showcase the young musicians and vocalists she likes to sponsor. Aoede's personal rooms are reserved for only herself, and her most trusted of servants and companions. They can be sealed off from the rest of the penthouse level with a massive marble door on hydraulic hinges, and Aoede has a private elevator in her section that leads down to the basement levels of the building.

Multiple guest rooms, dining areas, lounges, a wet bar, and even a pool that offers a vertigo inducing view of the city skyline are among the amenities that can be enjoyed by guests of Aoede. Other Psychic Vampires who come to visit their eldest sister will typically do so by flying in to land on her private balcony, away from the prying eyes of close-circuit cameras.

IMPERIAL STATE BUILDING:
Effectively identical to the Empire State Building IRL, the Imperial State Building is Noir York City's most famous of landmarks. This art-deco style skyscraper provides a mix of business and residential spaces. Richard Barrister keeps his private office here, on the floor rented out by his Barrister Media and Broadcasting Corporation, somewhere around the 50th Floor.

GREENWITCH VILLAGE CAFE:
Greenwitch Village is a neighborhood on the lower west side of Van Hattan island, close to the Devil's Oven. Post WW2 the neighborhood has become a hotspot for beatniks, artists, and wealthy kids playing at being revolutionary thinkers. Several small new-age bookstores can be found here, marking it as the territory of the Cult of the Horned Goddess. The Greenwitch Village Cafe is a coffee shop/bookstore that is owned by one of the higher ranking Druidesses of the cult, Gretchen Moss, who uses the venue both to provide a legitimate cover for her activities, and as a gathering place for Initiates and Followers who seek to socialize between the big quarterly celebrations. Featuring an open-mic for musicians and would-be poets, the Cafe is where Kelly Kyle hones her craft as a folk singer, and is where she first met Gretchen.

# Non-Player Characters:

## AOEDE
Reward: 45xp
CULT: Boeotian Penthouse Club
VAMPIRE? Yes
BODY 3
MIND 4
SPIRIT 4

| | |
|---|---|
| Agility+3 | Beauty+5 |
| Knowledge+5 | Perception+3 |
| Charisma+4 | Empathy+4 |
| Focus+2 | Art+5 |
| Languages+4 | Psychokinesis+5 |
| Telepathy+3 | Demonology+2 |

## AMANDA BRYCE
Reward: 25xp
CULT: Horned Goddess
VAMPIRE? No
BODY 2
MIND 3
SPIRIT 3

| | |
|---|---|
| Beauty+3 | Knowledge+2 |
| Perception+3 | Technology+2 |
| Charisma+3 | Focus+3 |
| Ranged+2 | Art+2 |
| Telepathy+1 | Demonology+2 |
| Metamorphosis+2 | |

## RICHARD BARRISTER
Reward: 25xp
CULT: Boeotian Penthouse Club
VAMPIRE? No
BODY 3
MIND 3
SPIRIT 2

| | |
|---|---|
| Beauty+1 | Strength+2 |
| Knowledge+4 | Perception+3 |
| Technology+3 | Boxing+2 |
| Ranged+2 | Art+3 |
| Languages+2 | Science+2 |
| Demonology+1 | |

## KELLY KYLE
Reward: 15xp
VAMPIRE? No
BODY 1
MIND 2
SPIRIT 3

| | |
|---|---|
| Beauty+3 | Knowledge+1 |
| Technology+1 | Charisma+3 |
| Empathy+2 | Melee+1 |
| Art+3 | Languages+1 |

## GRETCHEN MOSS
Reward: 30xp
CULT: Horned Goddess
VAMPIRE? No
BODY 2
MIND 3
SPIRIT 4

| | |
|---|---|
| Agility+3 | Beauty+3 |
| Knowledge+4 | Perception+2 |
| Charisma+3 | Focus+3 |
| Melee+2 | Art+1 |
| Science+1 | Psychokinesis+2 |
| Telepathy+1 | Demonology+2 |
| Metamorphosis+2 | Necromancy+1 |

## MARIA TUSCANO
Reward: 15xp
CULT: Horned Goddess
VAMPIRE? No
BODY 2
MIND 2
SPIRIT 2

| | |
|---|---|
| Beauty+1 | Knowledge+2 |
| Perception+4 | Empathy+3 |
| Focus+1 | Languages+1 |
| Clairvoyance+3 | |

## JAKE & HENRY LANGFORD

| | | |
|---|---|---|
| Reward: 10xp | CULT: Horned Goddess | VAMPIRE? No |
| BODY 3 | MIND 1 | SPIRIT 2 |
| Strength+2 | Perception+1 | Technology+2 |
| Boxing+2 | Melee+1 | Ranged+2 |

# Encounters:

TAILING AMANDA:

Following Amanda Bryce without her knowledge will require Hard difficulty stealth actions (Body+Agility) to successfully avoid being noticed by her. Each Character tailing her must make a separate roll once between destinations, unless they are traveling together in the same automobile or other vehicle. The driver will make a Mind+Technology roll at Hard difficulty to avoid being detected by the target. In both instances, a reasonable distance needs to be maintained between the target and those tailing them, or they will have to make an additional Very difficult stealth action.

Amanda spends most of her time at Aoede's Penthouse, but does have a small apartment of her own in Greenwitch Village, where she may go to make some phone calls, before heading to the Greenwitch Village Cafe to find Kelly Kyle. She will wait there until evening, when Kelly arrives to do a set at the open mic. Afterwards, Amanda will attempt to talk to Kelly, but her efforts will be hampered by the nosiness of Gretchen Moss. Amanda will eventually leave the Cafe, and wait in her car to follow Kelly Kyle to her home in Bronxlyn, where she will use her Telepathy to get Kelly to invite her inside for a drink.

## TARGET ACQUIRED:

Amanda will not have much luck, on her own, convincing Kelly Kyle to come back with her to Aoede's penthouse, despite promises of scheduling a meeting between her and "someone connected to the record industry with a lot of influence". She is aware that Amanda is some sort of rival to her girlfriend, Gretchen, higher up in the new age scene, and is resistant to her efforts to talk her into it. Player Characters will need to step in to help Amanda out with or without her knowledge. But one way or another, they will have to get the ripening artist to Aoede without causing her any harm. If she is under duress, or psychic influence, she will not be able to complete the song she has been working on.

Players will have to get creative on how they want to approach getting her to agree to come to Rosenvale Tower to meet Aoede. She is very loyal to Gretchen, and efforts to try to seduce her will have a difficulty of 20. Deceiving her with a convincing lie will be Hard, and an unconvincing lie is Very Hard.

After three failed attempts she will no longer be receptive to the Character's efforts to talk her into coming along with them.

THE SEARCH PARTY:

If and when Kelly Kyle is taken to meet Aoede at her penthouse, Gretchen Moss will immediately suspect Amanda Bryce had something to do with her sudden disappearance. After only a day or two, Gretchen will dispatch three of her loyal followers, Maria Tuscano, and the Langford brothers, to find Kelly and bring her back to Gretchen's home in Duchess. Maria will use her Clairvoyance to guide them to Rosenvale Tower, where they will keep an eye out for Amanda and any known accomplices. Jake is armed with a police baton, and Henry has a revolver with only 3 bullets in it.

Once in Aoede's hands, Kelly Kyle will fall under her influence and ignore any previous conflict she may have had with Amanda Bryce and the Player Characters, as long as she was undamaged. Health, Sanity, and Morale included. This would require Aoede to assert her telepathic influence more strongly, which would spoil Kelly's ability to make a work of genuine creative art.

Maria and the Langford brothers will attempt to attack and kidnap Amanda when she is seen leaving the building. They will do the same to the Characters if they had been seen by Gretchen at the Greenwitch Village Cafe.

# "Insatiable"

A new serial killer is on the loose in Van Hattan, but this is no Vampire Urge at work murdering the homeless and prostitutes. This new killer has been seducing wealthy and attractive men, and then brutally ripping their throats open and letting them bleed out. This is the work of a fledgling Vampiress who has become drunk on the beastial pleasures of becoming a creature of the night.

The Boeotian Penthouse Club wants her found and brought back to the home of her creator, before she forces the police to start asking uncomfortable questions about all the blood drained bodies that filter through the city morgue on a monthly basis.

Melpomene, the Muse of Tragedy, has dwelled in one of the older apartment towers in Upper Van Hattan since the 1910's, and is respected among her sisters in the Penthouse Club. She had been given the privilege of performing the Rite of Becoming to allow their lost sister, Calliope, to return to life in a new undead body.

The ritual, which took place on Christmas Eve of 1954, seemingly worked as intended, but Calliope had been gone from the mortal world for over two hundred years, adrift in the Lower Heavens as she recovered from a massive blow to her ego from Mneme. She has forgotten much of mortal ways, and has regressed to a semi-feral state where she needlessly hungers for blood and intercourse. She escaped from Melpomene's lair on the very next night, and has been sleeping in the subway tunnels beneath Van Hattan ever since, to avoid the sunlight. Her human memories inherited with her new body give her enough information to know where to find her preferred quarry, and how to get them to invite her to go home with them.

After several months of this, the police are starting to take a more active interest in this new serial killer than with most, with public pressure mounting on them to do something. Damn the poor and the sex workers, these are wealthy business-men loosing their lives. The Penthouse Club's influence over the Noir York Police Department has been neutralized by this "public" outcry on the news radio and television stations.

As it is considered normal for a newly reborn Psychic Vampire to take a few months to adjust to their new body and circumstances, the other Muses have not yet realized that it is once sweet Calliope who is behind the killings. They are convinced it must be the work of a Vampire Urge who was forced to take a woman's body, or one of the Hantu Belian vampires. None of them had ever been gone from the mortal world for as long as Calliope had, since they started taking human bodies to dwell in centuries ago. They did not remember how irrational they had been in those early days, how it took at least a century among humans to truly master their ways, and exert control over their mammalian brains. Calliope has forgotten how to do any of this, and she is thus ruled by her body's animal passions.

Only Melpomene knows the identity of the "Red Widow of Bull Street", and it falls to her to put an end to her rampage. Player Characters can be in her entourage, or otherwise contracted by Melpomene, to find Calliope before the police do and either bring her back to her Creator, or destroy her if she gives them no other alternative.

# Locations:

MELPOMENE'S LAIR:

Melpomene owns a small, 20-story apartment building built in the 1880's in Upper Van Hattan, in sight of Bronxlyn. The building is old and largely vacant. The tenants that do live here are all members of Melpomene's Inner Circle, Entourage, and loyal followers. The higher ranking among these have entire floors to themselves, but the top two floor of the building are Melpomene's private domain, filled with libraries and collected souvenirs and three indoor hydroponics labs. She also has a small greenhouse and garden area atop the building's roof, with a separate entrance from her levels to that used by service personnel. In the decades she has owned it she has installed numerous secret doors and hidden stairwells so that she can move about the building's interior unseen. These secret doors are Impossible to detect with a Mind+Perception action. There is at least 1 in every apartment unit in the building.

Melpomene keeps an office and a gymnasium on the second floor, where she will conduct meetings and rituals with her followers and vampire sisters. On the first floor, her followers are employed in the Charitable Organizations being run on the Penthouse Club's behalf.

THE HOT OVEN SWINGER'S LOUNGE:
This exclusive club for high society rollers is found on the outskirts of the Devil's Oven, north of Greenwitch Village. Characters who investigate the homes of one or more of the Red Widow's victims may discover paraphernalia from the Hot Oven Swinger's Lounge (Mind+Perception Hard difficulty). It is a Jazz Club that serves high class clientele who like to pretend they're being radical by spending an evening dancing to Jazz music. Calliope has managed to use her telepathic skill to bend the wills of one of the club's bouncers, a man named Lewis Tyson, and one of the waitresses, Vanessa Robinson.

The owner, bartender and host of the club is a Were-Cat known as Big Bill Freeman, who is aware of Calliope's use of his club as a hunting ground. He has remained quiet about this for three reasons:

1:He does not want to attract the attention of the NYPD to his very profitable drinking establishment.

2: He does not want to cause offense with the wealthy and powerful Boeotian Vampires.

3: He despises most of the people who patronize his club, and does not particularly mind if they perish.

# Non-Player Characters:

**MELPOMENE**
Reward: 45xp
CULT: Boeotian Penthouse Club
VAMPIRE? Yes
BODY 3
MIND 4
SPIRIT 3
Agility+3        Beauty+5
Knowledge+4   Perception+3
Technology+2    Charisma+2
Empathy+1       Focus+3
Ranged+1        Art+3

Languages+2     Science+4        Clairvoyance+1
Psychokinesis+3 Telepathy+2     Demonology+2
Metamorphosis+1          Necromancy+2

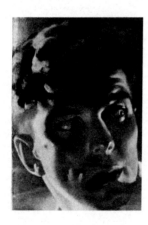

**DETECTIVE BRICK MALONE**
Reward: 20xp
CULT: None
VAMPIRE? No
BODY 2
MIND 3
SPIRIT 2
Agility+2        Strength+2
Knowledge+2    Perception+3
Technology+3    Boxing+2
Ranged+3        Science+3

## CALLIOPE/"VALERIE WELLES"
Reward: 15xp
CULT: None (Boeotian)
VAMPIRE? Yes
BODY 3
MIND 1
SPIRIT 2

| | |
|---|---|
| Agility+2 | Beauty+4 |
| Strength+1 | Perception+3 |
| Charisma+2 | Psychokinesis+1 |
| Telepathy+2 | |

## LEWIS TYSON
| Reward: 15xp | CULT: Hantu Belian | VAMPIRE? No |
|---|---|---|
| BODY 3 | MIND 2 | SPIRIT 2 |
| Strength+3 | Perception+3 | Focus+2 |
| Boxing+4 | Ranged+2 | Languages+1 |

## VANESSA ROBINSON
| Reward: 10xp | CULT: Hantu Belian | VAMPIRE? No |
|---|---|---|
| BODY 2 | MIND 2 | SPIRIT 2 |
| Agility+2 | Beauty+2 | Knowledge+1 |
| Charisma+2 | Empathy+2 | Art+1 |

## BIG BILL FREEMAN
| Reward: 20xp | CULT: Hantu Belian | VAMPIRE? Yes |
|---|---|---|
| BODY 3 | MIND 2 | SPIRIT 3 |
| Strength+2 | Knowledge+3 | Perception+3 |
| Charisma+1 | Focus+3 | Boxing+3 |
| Art+2 | Telepathy+1 | Demonology+2 |

# Encounters:

CRIME SCENES:
Several of the apartments where Calliope killed her prey are still closed off to the public. Characters who intrude on them can look for clues about who they were, where they worked, and whom they had contact with. It won't be until the second or third crime scene visited before any of the Player Characters start to notice the presence of matchbooks, napkins, or shot glasses featuring the logo of the Hot Oven Swinger's Lounge in each crime scene, with a Hard Mind+Perception action.

After visiting more than one crime scene and or visiting the city morgue, Detective Malone will approach the Characters to ask them their business, and then tail them afterwards. Characters will have to make a Body+Agility if on foot, or Mind+Technology if driving, Very difficult action to avoid being followed by Detective Malone. He will follow them from destination to destination until they succeed at ditching him. If they split up and go separate ways, Malone will follow whomever he would deem to be the "most shifty" out of the Character group.

He will intervene if he is witness to any criminal activity, and invite them to come visit him at his office in Precinct-01.

CITY MORGUE:
Gaining access to the bodies of the Red Widow's victims will be Very difficult, regardless if they'd rather use stealth or talk their way in. The bodies of the 13 men so far slain show all the expected hallmarks of a vampire attack, with a sloppy attempt to cut their throats after the fact to obscure the fang marks on their necks, and explain the bleeding. Their autopsy reports will indicate signs of sexual activity with a female partner just prior to their time of death, and that death was caused by physical trauma to the throat and jugular veins leading to massive blood-loss. There were no signs of struggle such as scratches, bruising, or broken nails.

POLICE DEPARTMENT:
Precinct-01 of the Noir York Police Department handles most of the high-profile cases in Van Hattan, and Brick Malone has been placed in charge of the investigation. Detailed files about the various victims have been assembled, and thus far, the running theory is that the Red Widow is perhaps a professional escort, or Uptown prostitute, who has gone over the edge due to some unknown abuse she had suffered. Because of this running assumption about the killer's profile, they have been focusing on the city's pimps and escort services, and missed the common thread between the victims of frequenting the Hot Oven Jazz Lounge.

## HOT OVEN JAZZ LOUNGE:

If the Characters stake-out the Hot Oven Jazz Club, they will eventually spot Calliope enter the club and begin her evening's hunt. If the Characters have spoken to Big Bill Freeman about the situation with the renegade fledgeling, it could also be arranged for him to call the Characters the next time she comes to the club.

If confronted, Calliope will refuse to listen to the Characters. If they persist in trying to talk to her, especially if they mention returning to Melpomene, she will move to leave the club, and telepathically order Lewis Tyson and Vanessa Robinson to attack the Characters who were talking to her.

If Calliope is allowed to leave the Lounge, she will use her telekinetic flight to flee down and alley way to the nearest subway entrance.

## THE SUBWAY TUNNELS:

Characters that attempt to find Calliope in the labyrinthian network of subway tunnels under Van Hattan will have to make periodic Mind+Perception actions at Impossible difficulty in order to find even a trace of Calliope's passage through that area. Finding her down here, if the characters were not in hot pursuit as she entered the tunnels, will require the use of Clairvoyance, at Hard difficulty.

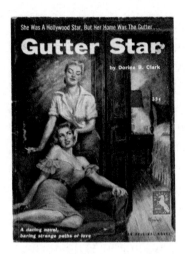

## "Gutter Star"

Polyhymnia has recently fed, and is now looking to replace her lost companion with a new protege to school in the arts of drama and comedy. While reading one of the local gossip magazines, Polyhymnia saw the solution to her problem: Agatha Harlow, a Noir York girl who went to Hollywood and somehow managed to land starring roles in a handful of popular detective and adventure films, has come home to care for her ailing mother in the Brooks.

Polyhymnia absolutely must have her!

She will promise Player Characters any number of things that may entice them, and are in her power to give, in order to get them to agree to go to the Brooks for her, find Agatha Harlow, and convince her to return to Van Hattan to be introduced to

Polyhymnia. The century-old Vampire knows she has plenty of time to steer young Miss Harlow's career in the direction she wants for her, so is not opposed to the Characters having to resort to the use of force if they must. Just leave no lasting harm, and bring her to Polyhymnia alive.

The truth about Agatha Harlow is that her mother is just fine, and doesn't need her help as a nursemaid. She's barely in her 50's. The problem young Agatha is facing is she has effectively blacklisted herself in Hollywood by turning down the advances of a well connected producer. She has been partying a lot since coming home, doing drugs and hanging around with illicit people. Finding her may require an evening or two of bar hopping and party crashing around the greater Noir York city area until she can finally be located.

Mind+Knowledge at Average difficulty to find a public bar or dance club where mid-to-high class clientele go to have fun. Once there, it will take a Spirit+Charisma action at Hard difficulty to learn the location of a nearby party.

Roll 2d6 when Characters reach a bar or party after the first. If both of the dice rolled are 1's, Agatha Harlow is there.

Convincing Agatha Harlow that Polyhymnia could help salvage her film career is a fairly Average task (Spirit+Charisma). Once back at Polyhymnia's studio, however, things may become more difficult. Agatha's experiences on the casting couch have put her on guard against many of the signals Polyhymnia is giving off when she meets her. Polyhymnia will want to deliver on results, and sends the Characters to visit with an off-Broadway producer, Jim Keller, to ensure Agatha will have a favorable audition in his next production.

It will come as a surprise to everyone when Agatha does not get the part. Jim Keller has been threatened by Agatha's former producer in Los Angeles, and cannot have Agatha cast in the production or be in violation of the Producer's Guild.

Polyhymnia will not be thwarted. Upon hearing this news, she will arrange with another one of her contacts on Broadway to set up an invitation for Harry Winston to come to Noir York to accept an award for Humanitarian of the Year, where the Characters will be waiting to make sure he eats his just desserts.

With Winston out of the way, Polyhymnia will guide Agatha through a string of Broadway hits followed by winning an Oscar for her return film performance, before finally feeding on her, and making it look like she committed suicide.

# Locations:

POLYHYMNIA'S STUDIO:
Polyhymnia lives in an underground apartment
beneath a massive studio complex in the Devil's
Oven, where she and her Inner Circle conduct
classes on dance, theater, and orchestral music. A
fine arts center financed through the Penthouse
Club on government grants for arts programs in the
inner cities. Polyhymnia keeps a private office near
the dance studio, where she hold private classes late
at night with her best students. A fair portion of
Broadway's talent has been schooled here, and it
has proven to be a rare opportunity for poor kids
from the Oven to have a chance at getting in the
spotlight.

THE HARLOW RESIDENCE:
Agatha's mother lives in an average run-down
house in the Brooks. Her daughter has not been
home since the night she arrived to dump her
luggage off in her old room. No amount of waiting
will lead to Agatha returning here. She will party
herself into the grave unless the Characters find her.
Looking for clues in Agatha's baggage will find,
with a  Very difficult Mind + Perception action, a
crumpled sheet of paper wedged in her suitcase. It is
a telegram to come to a meeting with "Mr. Winston"
dated four months ago in L.A..

THE OLD VAN HATTAN THEATER:
This vintage off-broadway theater in Upper Van Hattan is frequently staging plays and musicals, and is often sought out by actors who are looking to "get back to their roots" by performing in a lesser venue that still gives them access to the Van Hattan lifestyle. Jim Keller owns the theater and serves as its primary producer.

THE ROCKFORD BUILDING:
The awards show that Polyhymnia will arrange to have Harry Winston invited to will take place at the famous Rockford Building, where NCB Television Studios is broadcast from. Polyhymnia will make sure the Characters have full access to the building, as well as Mr. Winston's seating arrangements and point of exit. The Ceremony will take place in a large ballroom on the 2nd Floor of the building

After receiving his award, Winston will be directed by one of the show's ushers to exit via an elevator behind the curtains that will take him to the underground parking level. From here the Characters can intercept him, and do as they please. As long as he never speaks to anyone again, Melpomene will be satisfied that the job is finished, and young Agatha can get back to rebuilding her Hollywood career.

# Non-Player Characters:

**POLYHYMNIA**
Reward: 35xp
CULT: Boeotian Penthouse Club
VAMPIRE? Yes
BODY 4
MIND 3
SPIRIT 3

| | |
|---|---|
| Agility+4 | Beauty+3 |
| Strength+3 | Knowledge+1 |
| Perception+3 | Technology+1 |
| Charisma+3 | Empathy+5 |
| Focus+2 | Boxing+2 |

Psychokinesis+4  Telepathy+2      Metamorphosis+2

**AGATHA HARLOW**
Reward: 15xp
CULT: None
VAMPIRE? No
BODY 2
MIND 2
SPIRIT 3

| | |
|---|---|
| Agility+2 | Beauty+4 |
| Knowledge+1 | Technology+1 |
| Charisma+3 | Empathy+1 |
| Art+2 | Languages+1 |

## KATELYN POWERS
Reward: 25xp
CULT: None
VAMPIRE? No
BODY 1
MIND 3
SPIRIT 2

| | |
|---|---|
| Agility+4 | Beauty+2 |
| Knowledge+3 | Perception+4 |
| Technology+2 | Charisma+3 |
| Focus+3 | Art+1 |
| Languages+1 | Science+2 |

## JIM KELLER

| | | |
|---|---|---|
| Reward: 25xp | CULT: Penthouse Club | VAMPIRE? No |
| BODY 1 | MIND 3 | SPIRIT 2 |
| Knowledge+4 | Perception+2 | Technology+2 |
| Charisma+4 | Empathy+2 | Focus+3 |
| Ranged+1 | Art+5 | Languages+2 |

## HARRY WINSTON
Reward: 30xp
CULT: None
VAMPIRE? No
BODY 3
MIND 3
SPIRIT 3

| | |
|---|---|
| Strength+4 | Knowledge+5 |
| Perception+2 | Technology+4 |
| Charisma+4 | Focus+5 |
| Boxing+3 | Art+3 |

# Encounters:

MISSION NEWS:
At any point while hunting for Agatha, or in her company thereafter, a Character that succeeds at a Very difficult Mind+Perception action will notice that a woman is tailing Agatha. If confronted, the woman is revealed to be Katelyn Powers, a tabloid reporter for Mission News, a local paper. She is persistent about continuing to follow Agatha, and a Telepathic scan of her mind will reveal she knew Agatha back in High School. She can either be considered a nuisance, or could potentially be incorporated into a Player Character's entourage as a follower or companion.

THE AFTER-PARTY:
Polyhymnia has it set up that Winston will come out of the elevator into the parking garage with no security guards around. The characters can either take him by force, or try to convince him they are a security team sent to escort him to a limo. How they decide to "take care" of him as Polyhymnia wishes is up to the Player's discretion. Setting him free will greatly displease Polyhymnia, even if he agrees to whatever terms the Characters impose on him. Harry Winston is a wealthy and well connected man, and will issue many threats of retaliation mixed with promises of money, to try to bargain his way out of the situation he finds himself in.

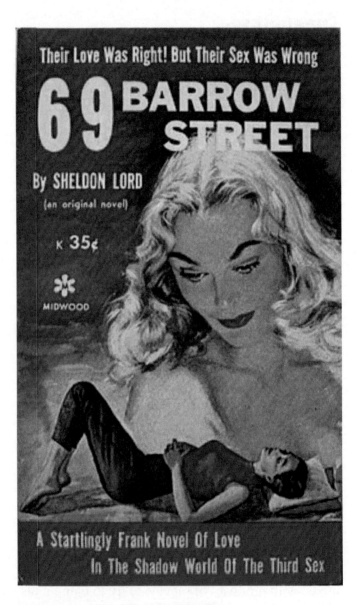

Their Love Was Right! But Their Sex Was Wrong

# 69 BARROW STREET

By SHELDON LORD

(an original novel)

K 35¢

MIDWOOD

A Startlingly Frank Novel Of Love
In The Shadow World Of The Third Sex

## HANTU BELIAN SOCIETY:

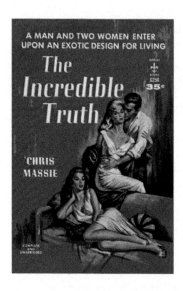

## "The Incredible Truth"

Diana Kitchener has spent years serving the Hantu Belian faithfully as their High Priestess in Bronxlyn. This is why it pains her to have to betray those that she has served to their fellow Were-Cats, for the heresy that they are committing:

They have allowed an outsider to witness their most sacred of rituals!

A mated pair of Were-Cats, Jenna and George Etheridge, have taken one of those harlot Druidesses as their companion-candidate, and have allowed her to participate in the sacred rite of the dream child. Diana wants to give them one last chance to come to their senses and send the Druidess away before she learns any more from them of the Hantu Belian ways. For this, she will recruit the Player Characters to find the mated Were-Cats and stop them before showing the Druidess the final component of the ritual to create a vampire. They only have 9 weeks remaining to stop them before the dream-child they conceived will need to be born into someone's dream.

Searching at Jenna's house in Bronxlyn will real the trio has left town, but no word was left with their servants as to where they went. Looking into Lacey Lovett's life will lead to her place of employment at Greenwitch Antiquities, a novelty shop frequented by members of the Cult of the Horned Goddess. Her co-workers could be tricked with a Hard Spirit + Charisma action into revealing that Lacey had left word with them that she was heading to upstate Noir York for the summer, to stay in a cabin in Finger Lakes National Park.

The Characters will have to prepare themselves for a road trip to the parkland, and then must find a way to identify the cabin their quarry is staying in. George Etheridge guards the cabin in question, while Lacey sleeps inside in a magical slumber, with Jenna no where to be seen.

Jenna has entered Lacey's dreamworld, to help her prepare a new ritual that would theoretically allow the Candidate whose mind would be devoured by the dream-child to preserve their identity and memories after the transformation, by having the mother carry the child to term within the Candidate's dreams. Whether or not this would work and allow Lacey to remain herself after becoming a Were-Cat is up to the Game Master to decide, but regardless of the ritual's viability, Jenna will have to be removed from Lacey's dream before she can be awakened and removed. This will require Telepathy, or the dream spells available to the Demonology skill.

George is prepared to fight to the death to prevent any interruption of Lacey's sleep-state, and if the Characters do have a way to enter her dream, they will have to battle past a variety of phantom guardians, who look like giant tigers made out of shifting clouds of mist, to reach the central dream where Lacey's consciousness resides, guarded by Jenna, who looks noticeably pregnant while in the dreamworld.

Finding a way to kidnap Lacey's sleeping body while George is distracted may be the only way to get to her without provoking a fight that could injure one of the Were-Cats, which Diana wants to avoid. Bringing Lacey to Diana will allow her to do the hard work of entering the Druidess' dreams and convincing Jenna of the error of her plan.

However, George will certainly be hot on the trail of anyone who dares to kidnap his wife's girlfriend. The Characters may need to stall him.

# Locations:

THE SECRET TEMPLE OF CAT-SITH:
The Secret Temple of Cat-Sith is hidden beneath a
butcher shop in old downtown Bronxlyn. The Hantu
Belian have used this place to conduct ceremonies
with their Inner Circles and Initiates since they first
came to Noir York, over 200 years ago. Here, High
Priestess Diana manages the day-to-day business of
running a secret underground cult of cat
worshippers, and is trusted by many of the Were-
Cats who dwell in Bronxlyn. Until recently, Jenna
Etheridge was the Were-Cat assigned to the Temple
to show up for ceremonies and holiday observances.
The entrance to the Temple is hidden next to a
dumpster in the alleyway behind the Butcher Shop.
Many stray cats lurk in the vicinity.

JENNA'S HOUSE:
Jenna lives in a decaying old house with boarded up
windows. She keeps an Initiate around named
David to keep an eye on the place during the
daytime, and stand guard while she sleeps. He is
annoyed with her for taking off on such short notice
with "that other woman", and will be Easy to
convince him to tell the Characters about Lacey's
place of employment in Greenwitch Village.

## GREENWITCH ANTIQUITIES:

Like the Greenwitch Village Cafe, this antiques and novelties shop is frequented by the women of the Cult of the Horned Dragon. Lacey Lovett works here, as an apprentice to one of the older Druidesses, Margaret Gray. Lacey is only an Initiate in the cult rankings, but has inflated her status while with the Etheridges. She met George Etheridge at the antique shop when he was looking for an appropriate gift to give to Jenna has part of his proposition for mating with her to create a new vampire. He knew of the shop's connections to the Druidesses and Lacey played along when he assumed her rank was higher than it was. Margaret Gray will willingly share information about Lacey's whereabouts, but will want to know why the Hantu Belian are looking for her.

## LAKESIDE CABIN:

George has rented his small entourage a modest but nice cabin overlooking the shore of one of the Finger Lakes in upstate Noir York. Information about renters could be found at the Park Registry Office, or the Characters could search the areas of the park marked as cabin and camping areas, which could take several days. For every cabin searched, roll 2d6. If both dice roll 1's, the correct cabin has been found. Most are spread apart, with narrow dirt road trails leading back to the entrance to the park. The landscape is mostly think, old-growth forest.

LACEY'S DREAMWORLD:
If any of the Characters know Dream Magic spells,
or are skilled enough with Telepathy, they can enter
and interact with Lacey's dreaming mind to locate
and retrieve Jenna. The dreamworld will be shed in
layers of scenery and memory as the characters
make their way forward to reach the center. There
are 5 layers the Characters will have to cross:

1st Layer: The dreamscape here resembles the
woods outside of the cabin, only darker, and with
larger and more menacing trees. A firelight in the
distance guides the way to the next level.

2nd Layer: Jenna's childhood bedroom when she
was 8 years old. There's shouting outside the door
as her father beats her mother savagely for letting
the tuna casserole get cold before he got home.
Opening the door will lead to the next level.

3rd Level: This layer looks like a recreation of
Jenna's college graduation ceremony, with all the
students in faculty in attendance, but all the
characters are naked. Getting behind the bleachers
to hide will open the next level.

4th Level: This level appears to be in the inside of
Greenwitch Antiquities, except the aisles are infinite
and twisting. Reaching the time clock will open the
final level.

5th Level: The Interior of the Cabin where Lacey sleeps, except the Characters find empty beds. Laying down in them reveals the Center of the Dreamworld.

The Center: This part of the dream looks like a rock and roll bar, with flashing lights and loud music coming from somewhere, and the sound of laughter and drunken merriment, but there is no one to be seen. The stage and the dance floors are empty. Only two women can be found here, sitting at the bar, having a conversation when the Characters approach them.

# Non-Player Characters:

**DIANA KITCHENER**
Reward: 20xp
CULT: Hantu Belian Society
VAMPIRE? No
BODY 2
MIND 2
SPIRIT 4

| | |
|---|---|
| Beauty+1 | Knowledge+2 |
| Perception+1 | Charisma+4 |
| Melee+1 | Art+2 |
| Languages+2 | Blessing+3 |
| Healing+2 | Demonology+2 |

## LACEY LOVETT
Reward: 25xp
CULT: Horned Goddess
VAMPIRE? No
BODY 2
MIND 2
SPIRIT 3

| | |
|---|---|
| Beauty+3 | Knowledge+3 |
| Technology+2 | Charisma+4 |
| Focus+3 | Melee+1 |
| Art+3 | Science+1 |
| Telepathy+2 | Demonology+3 |

## JENNA ETHERIDGE
Reward: 25xp
CULT: Hantu Belian Society
VAMPIRE? Yes
BODY 2
MIND 3
SPIRIT 4

| | |
|---|---|
| Agility+4 | Beauty+3 |
| Knowledge+1 | Perception+2 |
| Charisma+1 | Boxing+2 |
| Art+1 | Languages+2 |
| Telepathy+3 | Demonology+4 |
| Metamorphosis+2 | |

### GEORGE ETHERIDGE
Reward: 30xp
CULT: of Personality
VAMPIRE? Yes
BODY 3
MIND 3
SPIRIT 2

| | |
|---|---|
| Agility+3 | Strength+4 |
| Perception+3 | Technology+2 |
| Charisma+2 | Focus+3 |
| Boxing+3 | Melee+1 |
| Psychokinesis+1 | |
| Telepathy+1 | Demonology+4 |
| Metamorphosis+3 | |

### MARGARET GRAY
Reward: 25xp
CULT: Horned Goddess
VAMPIRE? No
BODY 2
MIND 4
SPIRIT 2

| | |
|---|---|
| Beauty+2 | Knowledge+4 |
| Perception+2 | Technology+2 |
| Focus+4 | Art+4 |
| Science+1 | Clairvoyance+1 |
| Telepathy+2 | Necromancy+3 |

## PHANTOM TIGER
Reward: 10xp
MIND 2
SPIRIT 3
Perception+3  Charisma+2
Empathy+3    Focus+2
ATTACK: Fear (Charisma) 1
morale damage
ATTACK: Horrid Vision
(Empathy) 1 sanity damage

# Encounters:

DREAM NAVIGATION:
Each layer of Lacey's dreamworld requires a Hard
Spirit+Empathy action to determine what leads to
the next level. Upon heading towards that level's
exit with the intent to leave, Phantom Tigers will
appear, 1 for every 2 Characters in the group who
have entered Lacey's dreams (rounding up). Once
the Phantoms have been defeated or chased away,
they will be able to move to the next level, and
begin the process again.

# "Unnatural"

A Were-Cat art thief has managed to trick her way into the entourage of the Psychic Vampire, Clio. Her target: a petrified cat from the Gobi Desert locked away in Clio's private museum of precious historical artifacts. Now she calls upon the Player Characters for assistance to pull off her heist against one of the oldest known vampires in all the world.

Clio has a fabulous ultra-modern condo downtown, but her private museum is concealed in a nondescript warehouse near the East Harbor in Lower Van Hattan, a stone's throw away from the Financial District. Clio's collection is famous in blackmarket art circles, and she frequently hosts viewings for international visitors, giving Clio the most far ranging sphere of influence of any of the original Muses living in Noir York. Esmerelda Cartagena has made two attempts at breaching Clio's security, but even in the form of a cat she failed to get inside. A friend had joked that she should try sleeping with the old Muse, and see if that would work. Esmerelda scoffed at first, but over time, the idea started to make more sense.

Thankfully the Psychic Vampires of the Boeotian Penthouse Club were accustomed to seeing Were-Cat Vampires crash their parties. Esmerelda easily inserted herself into one of Clio's more public museum exhibitions, and managed to draw the elder Muse's eye with some strategic use of Metamorphosis to make Esmerelda appear more like Clio's reported "type". They chatted some, and Clio did not question it when Esmerelda showed up a week later at one of her smaller parties held at her condo. For close to a year Esmerelda has gained Clio's trust and affection, and has now been along with her on three occasions to see her private collection in the warehouse.

Esmerelda's plan is fairly straightforward. She knows that a group of foreign art smugglers are coming to see the collection in a week's time, with an eye to sell her a stolen Rembrandt. She wants the Characters to intercept the smugglers at their hotel, and then impersonate them at the scheduled viewing at the warehouse. With Esmerelda in place at Clio's side, she will be able to use the copy of the key she made a wax mold of off Clio's personal keyring, to remove the petrified cat from its case while the Characters have Clio and her security guards distracted, pretending to haggle for the price of an original Rembrandt portrait of an obscure Dutch nobleman. Once the item is noticed to be missing, Esmerelda hopes to see the blame placed on the smugglers, and will slowly stop coming around Clio's condo as often, so as to not rouse any suspicion and cause problems between the Boeotians and the Hantu Belian.

## Locations:

THE EAST-SIDE DINER:
This small, 24-hour restaurant is only a few blocks away from Clio's warehouse, and is where Esmerelda will meet with the Characters to discuss the plan before sending them off to intercept the smugglers. Esmerelda selected the venue as its owners have no known connections to any of the city's vampire cults. The clientele are poor, hard-working people who are there to eat and not stick their noses in other patrons' business.

## THE HEIGHTON HOTEL:

This 5-Star Hotel is located in central Van Hattan, and is considered to be among the better hotels to be found in and around Noir York. The smugglers that are scheduled to meet with Clio at the end of the week are staying here in a suite on the 8th floor.

## WAREHOUSE 287:

On the freight registries, Warehouse 287 is marked for long-term storage of hundreds of pallets of self-sealing stem-bolts that have been stored there since the end of the war. The building is plain, and blends in with the other warehouses surrounding it in its section of the East Harbor district. Inside the Warehouse, the stem-bolt pallets are stacked in such a way as to make the warehouse appear full to capacity, while actually hiding a large area in the center of the building where Clio's private collection is stored. Besides the Harbor Security that patrols the area at night, Clio employs her own security team to keep watch on the site. 3 security officers with a pair of doberman guard-dogs are always on duty. CCTV cameras are positioned on the roof to cover all angles of entry.

Covered in sheets or secured in glass display cases, Clio has millions of dollars in illegal stolen paintings, statues, historical artifacts, and even a small intact dinosaur skeleton in her collection. The petrified cat is in one of the smaller display cases.

# Non-Player Characters:

## ESMERELDA CARTAGENA
Reward: 30xp
CULT: Hantu Belian Society
VAMPIRE? Yes
BODY 3
MIND 3
SPIRIT 3

| | |
|---|---|
| Agility+3 | Beauty+2 |
| Knowledge+3 | Perception+4 |
| Technology+4 | Charisma+2 |
| Focus+2 | Melee+1 |
| Art+4 | Science+1 |

Psychokinesis+2
Metamorphosis+2

## CLIO
Reward: 40xp
CULT: Boeotian Penthouse Club
VAMPIRE? Yes
BODY 3
MIND 5
SPIRIT 4

| | |
|---|---|
| Agility+2 | Beauty+5 |
| Strength+2 | Knowledge+5 |
| Perception+4 | Technology+3 |
| Charisma+2 | Focus+4 |
| Boxing+2 | Ranged+2 |
| Art+5 | Languages+4 |

| | | |
|---|---|---|
| Science+2 | Clairvoyance+1 | Psychokinesis+4 |
| Telepathy+3 | Demonology+1 | Necromancy+2 |

55

## ART SMUGGLERS

Reward: 20xp     CULT: None     VAMPIRE? No
BODY 3     MIND 2     SPIRIT 1
Strength+2     Perception+2     Technology+3
Boxing+2     Melee+2     Ranged+3
Art+3     Languages+2

## CLIO'S SECURITY GUARDS

Reward: 15xp     CULT: None     VAMPIRE? No
BODY 2     MIND 2     SPIRIT 2
Strength+2     Perception+4     Technology+2
Focus+4     Ranged+3

## MUUR KHAAN

Reward: 50xp
CULT: None
VAMPIRE? Yes
BODY 5
MIND 3
SPIRIT 4
Agility+3     Strength+3
Perception+3     Charisma+4
Focus+5     Boxing+4
Melee+5     Ranged+4
Psychokinesis+3
Telepathy+4     Blessing+3
Demonology+4
Metamorphosis+5

# Encounters:

HOTEL HIT JOB:

The smugglers are intentionally left vague as they will roughly match the number and description of the Player Characters who must replace them to meet with Clio. Characters will have to locate their room, and formulate a plan to neutralize them. At least one of the smugglers will have a revolver, the rest are armed with knives.

THE PRIVATE VIEWING:

The Character that is acting as the smugglers' spokesperson will have to succeed at a Hard Spirit + Charisma action to bluff their way through having a conversation with Clio as she shows them her collection. They may add their Art Skill bonus to this roll. The remaining characters will instead have to succeed at Hard Mind+Focus actions to keep their thoughts from betraying their true motives when scrutinized by Clio's telepathic scans. Failure on any of these actions will lead to the meeting being brought to an end prior to negotiations. Failure to keep their thoughts to themselves will cause Clio to call for her security to remove the Characters, and Esmerelda, from the warehouse. The security guards are armed with pistols, plus they have the two attack dogs.

HAGGLING FOR REMBRANDT:
To keep Clio and her guards distracted while Esmerelda uses Metamorphosis to cast a shrinking spell on the petrified cat, they will have to succeed at three different actions:

First, they must connive Clio they understand the value of stolen art with a Hard Mind+Art roll.

Second, they must convince Clio they were able to steal the Rembrandt and smuggle it out of Europe with a Hard Mind+Technology or Science roll.

Thirdly, they must convince Clio they are willing to sell her the painting at a realistic price with a Hard Mind + Art roll.

They may fail once at one of these attempts, and be allowed to make a second roll, but only the one time. Two failures will make Clio decide against buying the painting, and the meeting will end before Esmerelda has time to finish securing the petrified cat. Success and Clio will discuss how they will go about payment and delivery, giving Esmerelda the last few minutes she needs to finish and return to the group before her absence is noticed.

SCOT FREE:

If the Characters successfully negotiate their way through their encounter with Clio, they will all leave the warehouse afterwards as planned. Esmerelda will meet with them early the next evening to give them their pre-arranged payment at the East-Side Diner.

It will be almost a week before Clio returns to the warehouse to find the petrified cat has been stolen. She will send an assassin from her Inner Circle to find the smugglers, and depending on how the Characters dealt with them earlier, Clio may be given the impression that they were killed in their hotel room by whomever payed them to steal her artifact. Unless they made an effort to disguise themselves before meeting Clio, they will need to avoid running into her again, in case she recognizes them.

Meanwhile, Esmerelda may ask the Characters for further assistance, as back-up when she attempts to use a restorative spell on the now miniaturized statue. They will go to the Secret Temple of Cat-Sith to perform the spell. The restoration not only returns it to its original size, but it also transforms it into a living cat, briefly, before it shape shifts into a vampire with central-asian features, dressed as a steppeland nomad. A lost figure of Hantu Belian myth, the warlord Muur Khaan.

A CHANGE OF PLANS:

If the negotiations over the Rembrandt fail and the meeting ends before Esmerelda can get back to the group, she will rush up to the characters as the meeting breaks apart, and tell them there has been a "change in plans". She will then put the miniaturized petrified cat between her teeth, and shapeshift into her own cat form before dashing off towards the warehouse exit.

Clio will pursue Esmerelda, leaving the Characters to have to escape on their own from the guards and their dogs. If they manage to do so, they will be hunted by Clio's followers. Clio is not able to catch up with Esmerelda, who escapes to seek refuge at the Temple of Cat-Sith. Clio's agents will be sent to speak with the Hantu Belian cultists about this grave insult, while Clio herself visits her sister Muses to stir up their outrage on her behalf.

In the midst of all of this, Muur Khaan will be restored by Esmerelda, without the Characters around to influence him after he emerges from his petrified state. He will likely seize control of the Temple, and declare himself as lord of the Were-Cats once more. It will take some time to find a translator who can understand him, so the ripples this will send through the Hantu Belian Society will be delayed by a week or more. Male Were-Cats in particular will start to flock to the city to pledge themselves to him, shifting the cult's balance.

## THE KING OF CATS:

Muur Khaan has been frozen in stone form for over 700 years when Esmerelda frees him from his imprisonment. Long ago, he had commanded a horde of his own under the banners of the great Chinggis Khaan, waging constant war against the peoples of Northwestern China at the eastern end of the Silk Road. He was as fearsome as the Raksasha of old, and was crowned as High King of all the scattered Were-Cats who roamed the Earth during that age. His reign of terror was finally brought to an end by a sorcerer from the Shao-Lin School, who ambushed Muur Khaan's war party while it crossed the Gobi Desert.

Muur Khaan is said to have taken his feline shape to avoid the sorcerer's magical attacks, which still overpowered him, turning him to stone to be trapped forever in a conscious void. The sorcerer and his mercenaries took the statue of Muur Khaan and set off to return to the Shao-Lin Temple, but survivors from Muur Khaan's entourage had rallied more of the Khaan's warriors, and they counter-attacked the sorcerer's force before they could reach the desert border. Both the sorcerer, and his mercenaries, were slaughtered, but the petrified form of Muur Khaan was lost in the fighting, and wasn't found until 650 years had gone by, and it was discovered by an American archeologist.

**CULT OF THE HORNED GODDESS**

The Vernal Equinox celebration draws near, and the Druidesses of the Cult of the Horned Goddess have gathered to discuss the usual business of preparing for the micro-festival in Center Park, and to select who will receive the honor of being their next virgin sacrifice to the "Vampire Tree" hidden away in Duchess. One of the Druidesses, Sally Quinn, who works as a teacher in Greenwitch Village High School, has someone in mind who fits the qualifications: Beautiful. Believes in the Horned Goddess. And her virginity is still intact.

With the Council's approval, the girl will be informed that she has been chosen to take part in the Ritual of Year's Renewal at the culmination of the

Vernal celebrations. The Characters will be assigned to keep an eye on the girl for the next few weeks, until the day of the festival when she is to be escorted to the warehouse in Duchess, instead of Center Park.

The assignment doesn't seem all that bad. Rebecca Carmichael, as she is named, lives with her parents in an apartment in Greenwitch, and goes to school and doesn't skip class, and does all the normal things you'd expect from a straight-laced 17 year old in the 1950's. It's actually rather boring, but if you'd like to spice things up, a week or so into the assignment, the Characters will notice that they are being watched by someone else if they succeed at a Very difficult Mind+Perception action.

Rebecca is being used as bait by her father, who is a member of the Knights of the Temple of the Blood of Christ Divine. He has grown to suspect that Rebecca's History teacher practices some sort of vampiric witchcraft, and told his daughter to play along as if she too believed in it. Ironically, she now kind of does, but if the Characters never notice the Knight watching them watch her, they will follow the Characters when they finally escort Rebecca to the cult's warehouse in Duchess, where they will interrupt the Ritual of Year's Renewal, and set fire to the old tree while rescuing Rebecca. The experience will kill any further curiosity about pagan beliefs that she may harbor.

If the Characters discover the involvement of the Knights of Christ Divine, they will be able to prevent the destruction of the vampire tree, but at the cost of having to face Father Carmichael and his vampire hunters by themselves.

Father Carmichael's squad of hunters have Divine skills on their side, and are over-equipped for the situation, as they expect to be fighting vampires, and not witches, if and when they go to rescue Rebecca on the equinox. The Druidesses' only advantage is their skills in the other magical schools, but caught unprepared, many members of the Druidess Inner Circle of the cult will be lost to gunfire. That the Knights will be facing at least 7 or more Druidesses and their most favored Initiates, the Player Characters may only have to deal with one or two of them to be able to escape the Warehouse before it catches on fire as the tree burns, depending on the size of the Player Group.

Realizing that the women gathered at the warehouse to witness Rebecca's sacrifice are not vampires, Father Michaels may want one or more of the survivors taken prisoner, to be interrogated at their hidden temple beneath a seminary school.

Catching the Knights early-on, before the equinox, is probably the only way to prevent this from happening, unless the Players come up with a brilliant plan to defend the tree.

# Locations:

## THE CARMICHAEL RESIDENCE:
The Carmichael family lives in a modest apartment on the 3rd floor of a five-story building on a nice street in Greenwitch Village, like some nightmare sitcom brought to life. The street and alleys are clean, the neighbors friendly. Characters who can be seen hanging around the area at night may have random strangers come up to them and offer them some coffee, just to be nice.

## THE CONDEMNED WAREHOUSE:
This old warehouse has been condemned for years, and is owned by a Trust placed under the control of the members of the Inner Circle of the Cult of the Horned Goddess. It looks like its about to fall apart in a cloud of rust, and no one goes near it. This is where the Druidesses keep the old dead tree they imported from Gotland to serve as their prop to keep the real vampires at bay. It is a gnarled and twisted old oak, which has been planted in the center of the warehouse floor. It is stained a dark color around its waist from the blood of the hundreds of girls sacrificed upon it over the years since it was brought to this place. It has no real power, and yet, even those who know this feel its presence, dominating the room with its twisted yer somehow charismatic appearance.

# Non-Player Characters:

### SALLY QUINN
Reward: 35xp
CULT: Horned Goddess
VAMPIRE? No
BODY 2
MIND 3
SPIRIT 3

| | |
|---|---|
| Beauty+3 | Strength+2 |
| Knowledge+4 | Technology+3 |
| Charisma+3 | Empathy+2 |
| Boxing+3 | Melee+2 |
| Languages+2 | Science+3 |
| Telepathy+1 | Exorcism+2 |
| Healing+3 | Necromancy+2 |

### REBECCA CARMICHAEL
Reward: 10xp
CULT: None
VAMPIRE? No
BODY 1
MIND 2
SPIRIT 2

| | |
|---|---|
| Agility+1 | Beauty+2 |
| Knowledge+1 | Perception+1 |
| Technology+1 | Focus+2 |
| Ranged+1 | Science+1 |

## FATHER STONE CARMICHAEL

Reward: 30xp
CULT: Knights of Christ Divine
VAMPIRE? No
BODY 4
MIND 2
SPIRIT 3

| | |
|---|---|
| Agility+1 | Strength+5 |
| Knowledge+1 | Perception+2 |
| Technology+3 | Charisma+1 |
| Focus+3 | Boxing+4 |
| Melee+3 | Ranged+2 |
| Languages+1 | Blessing+2 |
| Exorcism+1 | Healing+1 |

## WENDY CARMICHAEL

Reward: 20xp
CULT: None
VAMPIRE? No
BODY 2
MIND 2
SPIRIT 3

| | |
|---|---|
| Beauty+2 | Strength+2 |
| Perception+4 | Technology+2 |
| Empathy+4 | Focus+3 |
| Ranged+2 | Blessing+1 |

## VAMPIRE HUNTER SQUAD
Reward: 15xp    CULT: Blood Knights    VAMPIRE? No
BODY 2          MIND 1                 SPIRIT 3
Strength+1      Knowledge+1            Perception+3
Technology+2    Focus+2                Melee+2
Ranged+1        Exorcism+2             Healing+1

## RANDOM DRUIDESSES
Reward: 15xp         CULT: Horned Goddess    VAMPIRE? No
BODY 2              MIND 3                   SPIRIT 2
Agility+2           Beauty+2                 Knowledge+2
Perception+1        Technology+1             Melee+1
Psychokinesis+2 Healing+2                    Necromancy+2

## RANDOM INITIATES
Reward: 5xp         CULT: Horned Goddess    VAMPIRE? No
BODY 2             MIND 2                   SPIRIT 2
Beauty+1           Technology+1             Melee+1
Psychokinesis+2

# Encounters:

WHO WATCHES THE WATCHERS:
If the Characters spot the Knights watching them, they will have to catch Roger and Steven, who flee across the rooftop they were on when spotted. The Characters can fly up to the roof if they have points in Psychokinesis, or they can try to catch the two strange men as they flee down the stairwell. Neither have their vampire gear on, so they at best have jackets that give them Padded Armor protection, and Roger will have a revolver, and Steven will have a knife. If their Morale is broken they will reveal who sent them to spy on the Characters.

THE HIT SQUAD:

Father Carmichael is a retired Navy Chaplain who served in the Pacific during WW2. He has adapted the military tactics he had observed in action, turning his small team of vampire hunter wannabes into an effective paramilitary force, equipped with both bullet proof vests, and a helmet that covers their face and upper neck, modified from prototype racing helmets. In combination that gives them Armor protection equal to that of "Magical" (Very difficult). They are also equipped with Crossbows, and each member of the squad carries a hammer and a wooden stake. Some may have water balloons filled with Holy Water, but these do no damage if struck by one. Optionally it may impart the effects of a random blessing upon the Character, selected by the Game Master, that lasts until the next sunset.

They may also have some normal equipment, such as a revolver, knife, or baseball bat (club). Father Carmichael carries a hacksaw with him to remove the heads of any vampires they slay, and one of the other Knights will be carrying some rope, to tie up the last surviving vampire after they clean out the rest of their nest. Father Carmichael will also provide two of his men with Machine Guns, to sweep out any mortal followers, and weaken the vampire's healing abilities.

Including Father Carmichael, there are 5 Knights total in his Squad. The names of his teammates are Roger, Steven, Patrick, and Jeremy. His wife, Wendy, will often wait out in the car for him to finish up with whatever mission he is on.

DAY OF THE EQUINOX:
If the Knights of the Temple of the Blood of Christ Divine are not discovered watching the Characters, or following them as they take Rebecca to Duchess, their attack on the ceremony being conducted inside the Warehouse will go off without warning. Carmichael and his squad will have a full round to open fire on the gathered Druidesses before the Characters can take action.

There will be up to 9 Druidesses in attendance. Druidess Characters from previous adventures can make an appearance here, at the Game Master's discretion, but there will still be up to 5 additional Random Druidess NPCs and their Initiates in attendance when the Knights attack. Less if any of the Player Characters are themselves a low ranking Druidess.

The two squad members who are not equipped with machine guns will instead be carrying a molotov cocktail. It will take them a full turn to light it, before they can throw it at the tree on the next round. They are under orders to wait until Carmichael has untied his daughter from the tree.

# BONUS GALLERY

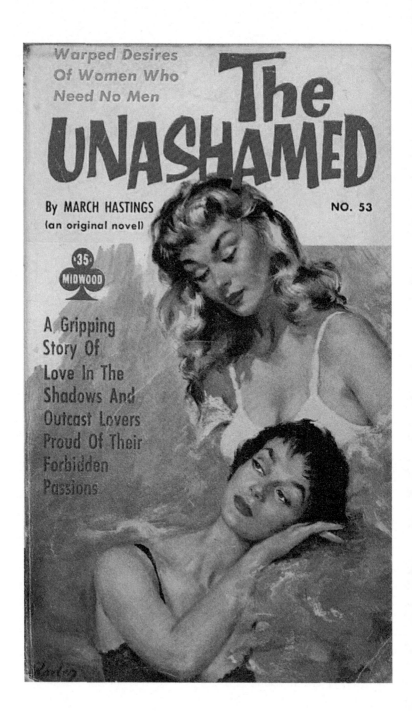

Warped Desires
Of Women Who
Need No Men

# The UNASHAMED

By MARCH HASTINGS

NO. 53

(an original novel)

35¢
MIDWOOD

A Gripping
Story Of
Love In The
Shadows And
Outcast Lovers
Proud Of Their
Forbidden
Passions

A STORY OF MEDITERRANEAN DEVIATES
THAT PALES *LA DOLCE VITA*...

# STRANGE SEDUCTION

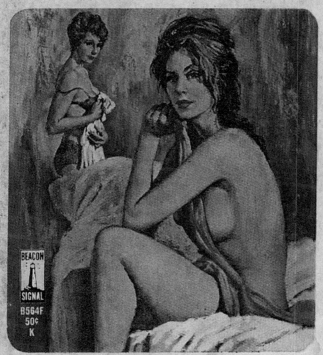

BEACON
SIGNAL
B564F
50¢
K

## ARTHUR ADLON

WHEN REPORTER BRIAN MERRIT TOOK THE ASSIGN-
MENT TO INVESTIGATE THE WILD TALES COMING
FROM THE ISLE OF HYERES ... HE DIDN'T KNOW
HIS OWN GIRL WAS INVOLVED ... *AND THAT HE
WOULD BE FORCED TO WATCH HER CORRUPTION AT
THE HANDS OF A BEAUTIFUL BUT WARPED WOMAN!*
A BOLD NOVEL OF DEVIATE LIFE WHICH PULLS NO PUNCHES

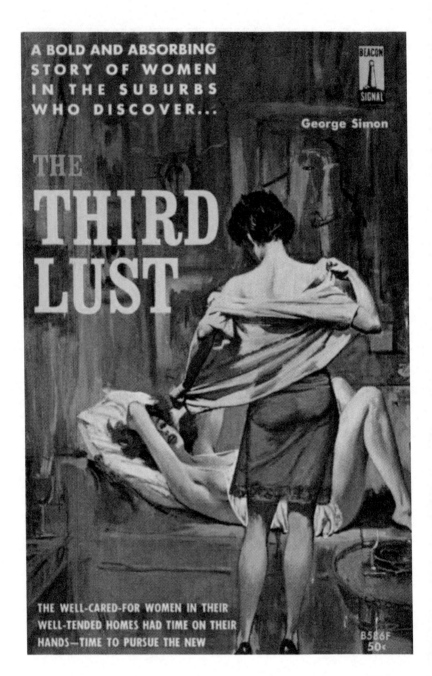

A BOLD AND ABSORBING
STORY OF WOMEN
IN THE SUBURBS
WHO DISCOVER...

BEACON SIGNAL

George Simon

THE
THIRD
LUST

THE WELL-CARED-FOR WOMEN IN THEIR
WELL-TENDED HOMES HAD TIME ON THEIR
HANDS—TIME TO PURSUE THE NEW

B586F
50¢

202

MONARCH BOOKS

35¢

The Amorous Adventures Of A Luscious
Model On Her Way To Success

# DEBBIE

## Paul Daniels

First Publication Anywhere

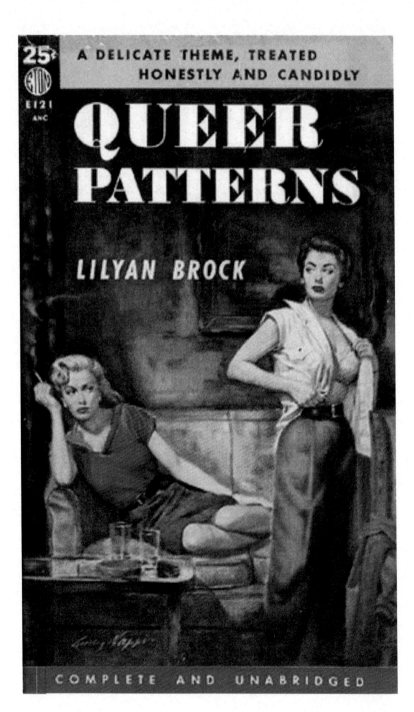

25¢

A DELICATE THEME, TREATED
HONESTLY AND CANDIDLY

E121
ANC

# QUEER PATTERNS

## LILYAN BROCK

COMPLETE AND UNABRIDGED

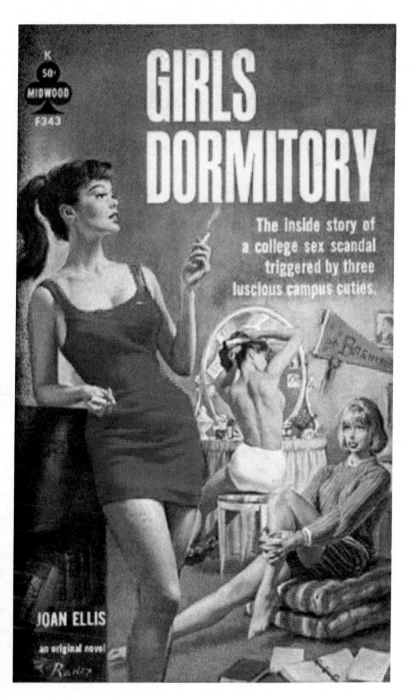

GIRLS DORMITORY

The inside story of a college sex scandal triggered by three luscious campus cuties.

K
50¢
MIDWOOD
F343

JOAN ELLIS
an original novel

Printed in Great Britain
by Amazon

39128268R00046